marley zermeno ♥
–gladys

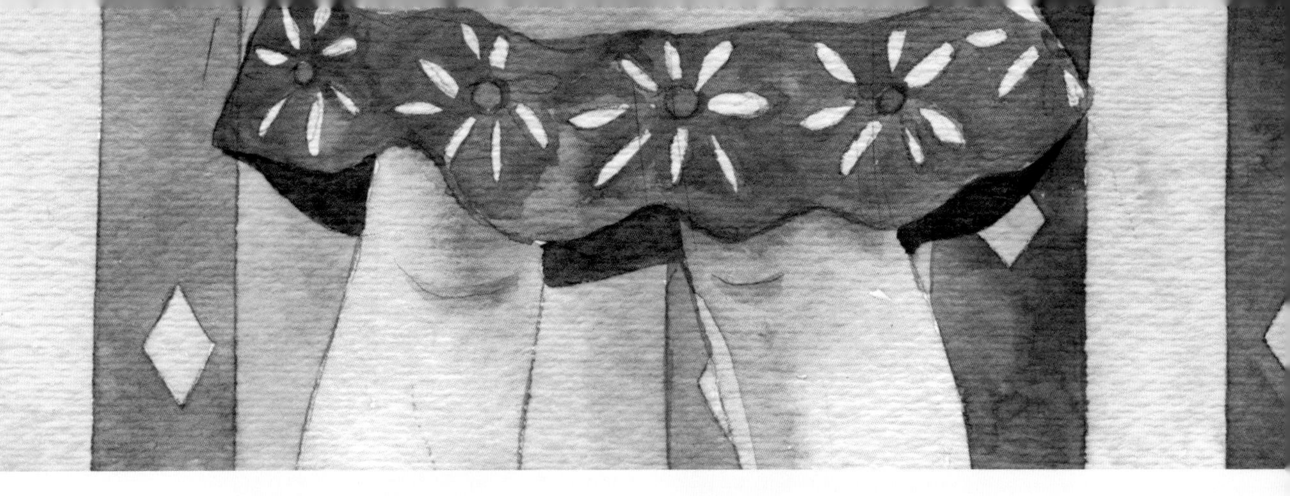

Rubber Shoes...

A lesson in gratitude

Los zapatos de goma...

una lección de gratitud

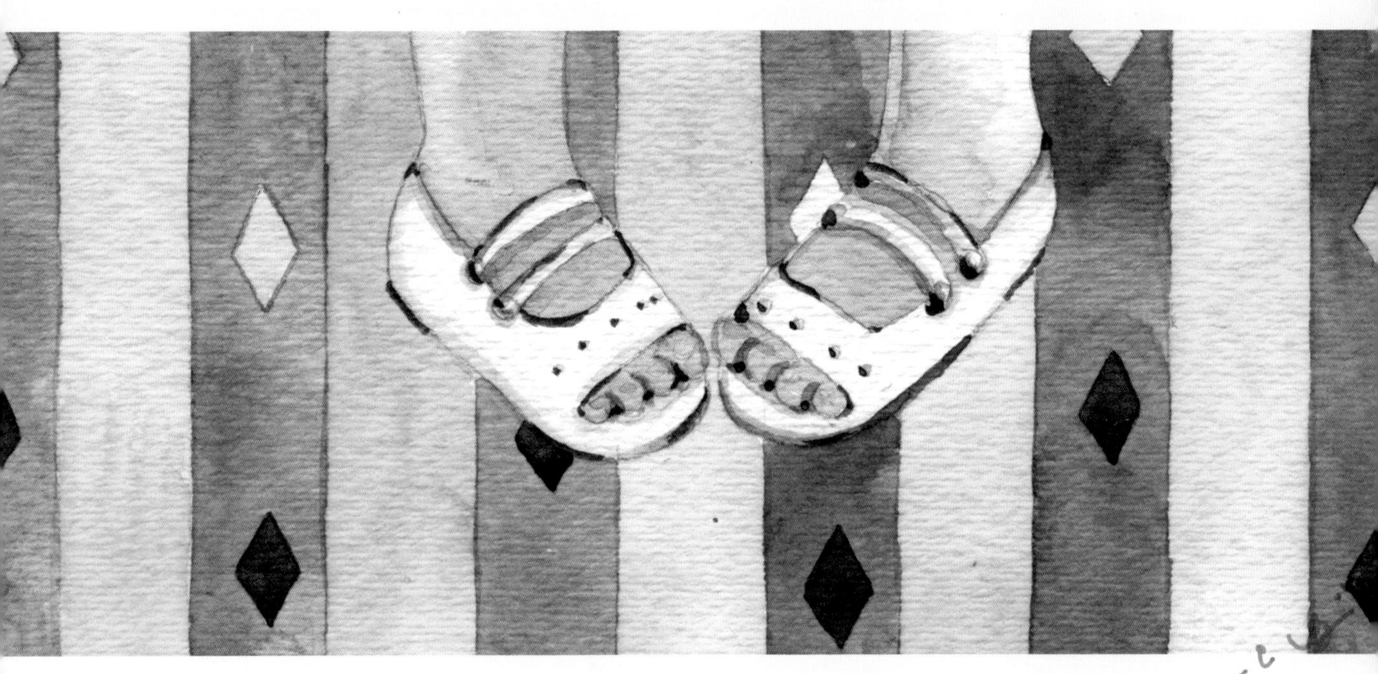

by/por Gladys Elizabeth Barbieri
illustrations by/ilustrado por Lina Safar
translated by/traducido por Liliana Cosentino

Publishers Cataloging-in-Publication Data

Barbieri, Gladys Elizabeth.
Rubber shoes : a lesson in gratitude / by Gladys Elizabeth Barbieri ; illustrations by Lina Safar ; translated by Liliana Cosentino = Los zapatos de goma : una lección de gratitud / por Gladys Elizabeth Barbieri ; ilustrado por Lina Safar ; traducido por Liliana Cosentino.
p. cm.
In English and Spanish.
Summary: Gladys Elizabeth is very disappointed with the new shoes her mother picks out for her. After trying unsuccessfully to rid herself of the shoes, she is taught a lesson in gratitude that changes her feelings about them.
ISBN-13: 978-1-60131-078-1
[1. Gratitude—Juvenile fiction. 2. Shoes—Juvenile fiction. 3. Bilingual books—Juvenile fiction.] I. Safar, Lina, ill. II. Title. III. Title: Los zapatos de goma : una lección de gratitud.
2010942106

Printed and bound in the United States of America

115 Bluebill Drive
Savannah, GA 31419
United States
(888) 300-1961

www.chuchosbooks.com
Rubber Shoes...a lesson in gratitude
Los zapatos de goma...una lección de gratitud

Winner of the
Moonbeam Children's Book Award:
Gold Medal Winner for Spanish Language Book 2011

This book was published with the assistance of the helpful folks at DragonPencil.com

CPSIA facility code: BP 310320

For my mother,
Sylvia.
Para mi mamá,
Sylvia.

"Where are we going, Mami?" I ask as I try to keep up with my mom's brisk pace.
"To buy you a new pair of shoes."

—¿A dónde vamos, mami?
—le pregunto mientras intento seguir sus ágiles pasos.
—A comprarte zapatos nuevos.

Did I hear right? Did my mom say we're going to buy me a new pair of shoes? "Yahoo!" I shout with joy. "New shoes!"

«¿Oí bien? ¿Zapatos nuevos para mí?»

—¡Viva, viva —grito de felicidad—, zapatos nuevos!

As we cross the busy street, my mom firmly holds my hand. My hand begins to feel sore from her tight grip. But I don't even care, because all I can think about are my new shoes.

Para cruzar una transitada calle, mamá me toma de la mano tan fuerte que me hace doler. Pero no me importa, ¡solo puedo pensar en mis zapatos nuevos!

Maybe I'll get shiny black shoes like Marilyn Jane, my best friend in the whole wide world.

Tal vez sean brillantes y negros como los de Marilyn Jane, mi mejor amiga...

Or perhaps I'll get sparkly white sandals like Nicky's . . .

O quizá sean sandalias blancas y centelleantes como las de Nicky...

Or ruby red slippers like Dorothy's. . .

O zapatillas de color rubí como las de Dorothy...

As I'm lost in my thoughts, I feel my mom fixing my not-so-fabulous bowl-cut hairdo (something I'll have to change soon). But for now, I think of only one thing: my new shoes.

Me dejo llevar por la fantasía y siento que mi mamá intenta acomodarme la melena taza. Tendré que cambiar pronto este feo peinado, pero ya me ocuparé de eso, por ahora, puedo pensar en una sola cosa: mis zapatos nuevos.

And just as we enter the shoe store, I see the most perfect shoes for me.
"Those, Mami!" I yell as I point to the pink ballet slippers.
"Those are just perfect!"

En cuanto entramos a la zapatería, veo los zapatos ideales para mí.
—¡Esas, mami! —grito entusiasmada señalando unas zapatillas de baile rosadas—. ¡Esas son perfectas!

My mom follows the direction
of my finger and makes an
expression that I can't figure out.
And with a heavy sigh she quietly
says, "Those are too expensive,
Gladys Elizabeth."
"Too expensive?" I question.

*Mi mamá sigue la
dirección de mi dedo y hace
un gesto que no entiendo.
—Son muy caras, Gladys
Elizabeth —me dice en voz
baja y suspira con tristeza.
—¿Muy caras?*

I quickly glance over the assortment of shoes. I see my mom pick a pair of shoes. They are the ugliest shoes with thick rubber soles and a red tag that reads "SALE." At that moment, I just want to hide and pretend to be invisible.

Ojeo el surtido de zapatos y veo que ella escoge un par con una etiqueta roja que dice «OFERTA». Nunca vi zapatos más horribles que esos y ¡con suela de goma gruesa! En este momento, lo único que quiero es esconderme y desaparecer.

As I try on the ugly rubber shoes, I try to make my mom understand that these are the worst shoes in the world. Doesn't she know that ballerinas don't wear rubber shoes?

Mientras me los pruebo, trato de hacerle entender que son los zapatos más feos del mundo. ¿Acaso no sabe que las bailarinas no usan zapatos de goma?

The next day at school, I pretend to be invisible, in the hopes that nobody will notice my ugly rubber shoes that my mom bought for me on SALE.

Al día siguiente en la escuela, finjo que soy invisible con la esperanza de que nadie se fije en los espantosos zapatos de goma que mi mamá me compró en OFERTA.

"Hi Gladys," Marilyn Jane greets me as I walk right past her.

"Don't talk to me, because I'm invisible and you are ruining it," I dryly reply.

—Hola, Gladys —me saluda Marilyn Jane cuando paso por al lado.

—No me hables porque soy invisible y vas a arruinar todo —le respondo secamente.

As soon as I get home from school,
I go to my room to make a weeklong plan
to rid myself of these shoes.

No bien vuelvo a casa, me voy a mi cuarto a idear un plan para deshacerme de los zapatos en una semana como máximo. Y lo pongo en práctica sin dudar.

On Monday, I rub the bottoms of my rubber shoes as hard as I can on the sidewalk. Unfortunately, I quickly learn that these shoes are not only ugly, but super-duper sturdy.

El lunes, me dedico a restregar con fuerza la suela de goma contra la acera. Desafortunadamente, compruebo enseguida que los zapatos no solo son horribles, sino superresistentes.

On Tuesday, I throw them in a puddle of mud, only to find that my mom can clean anything and that time-out is no fun.

El martes, los arrojo en un charco de lodo y lo único que descubro es que mi mamá puede limpiar cualquier cosa y que estar castigada no es nada divertido.

On Wednesday, my little sister rides her bike across my shoes over and over again. That doesn't work either.

El miércoles, mi hermanita pasa con la bicicleta por encima de ellos una y otra vez. Pero tampoco sirve.

On Thursday, I throw them over the fence and tell my mom that aliens took my shoes for a science experiment. In the middle of my fibbing, our neighbor appears at the front door with my rubber shoes in her hand. Did I mention that time-out is no fun?

El jueves, los tiro del otro lado de la cerca y le explico a mi mamá que los marcianos me los quitaron porque deseaban hacer un experimento científico. Mientras trato de simular convicción para ocultar mi mentira, la vecina aparece en la puerta de casa con los zapatos de goma en la mano. ¿Ya dije que estar castigada no es divertido?

On Friday, at the risk of spending the rest of my life in time-out, I decide to get rid of my weeklong plan to destroy my rubber shoes.

El viernes, a riesgo de pasar el resto de mi vida castigada, decido abandonar el plan para destruir los zapatos de goma.

Then one miraculous day, I put on my shoes and they do not fit! They are too small and that is the honest truth.

¡Hasta que un día milagroso, me pongo los zapatos y no me entran! Son muy pequeños, de verdad, ¡es la pura verdad!

Once again, we make our way down to the shoe store. But instead of arriving at the shoe store, we end up someplace else.

Entonces volvemos a salir con mamá para ir a la zapatería. Pero terminamos en otro lugar.

"Mami, what are we doing here? Let's go buy my new shoes," I say. Annoyed that my shoe-shopping experience is being interrupted, I begin to fidget. My mom sternly squeezes my hand and gives me the you're-going-to-get-it look.

—¿Qué hacemos aquí? ¡Tenemos que ir a comprar los zapatos! —protesto por la demora. Para entretenerme, empiezo a jugar. Mi mamá me da un apretón en la mano y me amenaza con la mirada: ¡¡Ya vas a ver lo que te espera!!

I then notice a little girl in tattered clothes who is a little bit smaller than me. My mom hands her a paper bag, and I watch the little girl pull out my old and ugly rubber shoes. But unlike me, who didn't like these rubber shoes, she smiles brightly as she puts them on.

De pronto advierto a una niña un poco más pequeña que yo, vestida con ropa muy gastada. Mi mamá le entrega una bolsa de papel, y la niñita saca mis zapatos de goma viejos y feos. A diferencia de mí, a ella le brilla la sonrisa en el rostro cuando se los pone.

The little girl jumps up and down and gives my mom a big hug. However, for some odd reason, I don't feel as excited as the little girl and once again I pretend to be invisible.

Salta de alegría y le da un abrazo enorme a mi mamá. Por una extraña razón, yo no me siento tan emocionada y una vez más finjo ser invisible.

As we walk out, my mom grabs my hand and we head over to the shoe store. Yet this time, my enthusiasm for my new shoes is not that great anymore.

Salimos del lugar y, entonces sí, vamos a la zapatería. Pero ahora mi entusiasmo por los zapatos nuevos ya no es tan grande.

The pink ballet shoes are still on display. "Well, aren't you going to show me the shoes that you want?" my mom gently teases.

Still not knowing why I feel sad, I whisper, "That's okay, Mami, you can pick them out."

Las zapatillas de baile rosadas todavía están en exhibición.

—Bueno, ¿no vas a mostrarme los zapatos que quieres? —bromea mi mamá con ternura.

—No, mami, escójalos usted —le respondo en un susurro, sin entender aún por qué estoy tan triste.

My mom gently squeezes my hand and kisses my forehead. However, all I can think about is the little girl jumping up and down. Perhaps my rubber shoes weren't so bad after all.

Me aprieta la mano cariñosamente y me besa la frente. No puedo dejar de pensar en la niñita, que saltaba de alegría. Tal vez mis zapatos de goma no estaban tan mal.

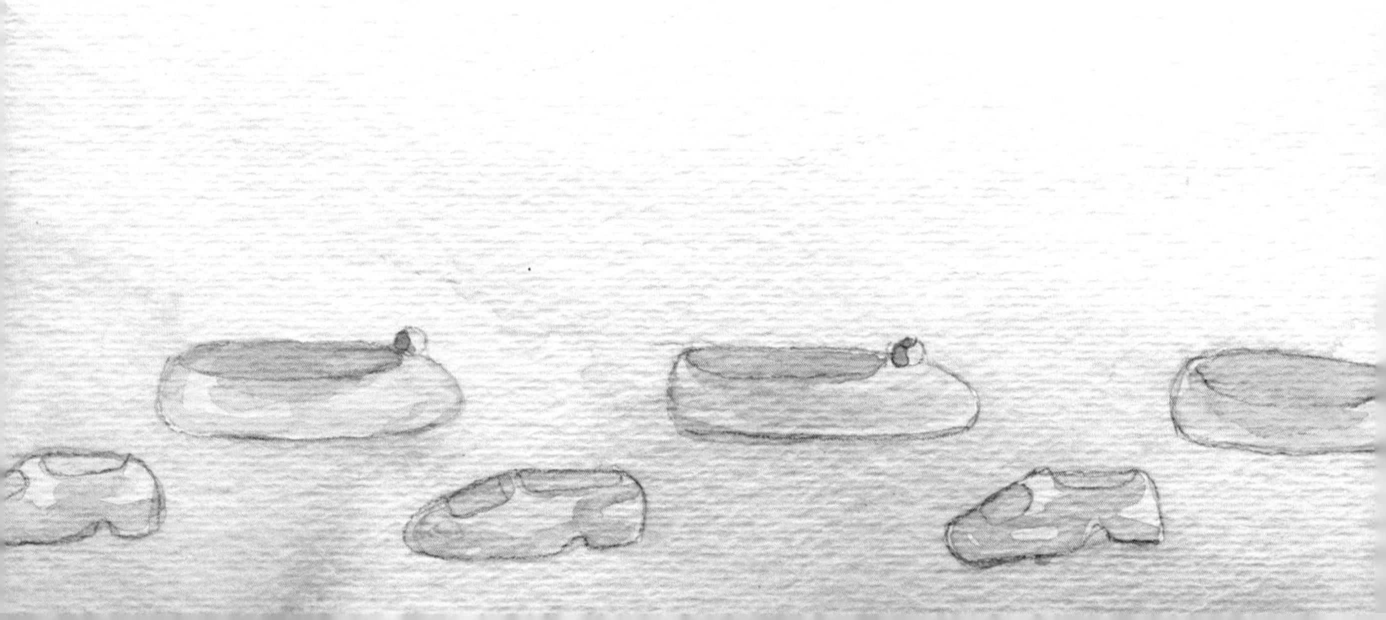

Gladys Elizabeth Barbieri is a first grade teacher in the Lennox School District: an unincorporated 1.3 square mile community that is underneath the LAX flightpath! She received her B.A. in Communications from the University of San Francisco and her M.A. in Elementary Education from Loyola Marymount University in Los Angeles. Because her parents immigrated to this country; her father from Nicaragua and her mother from El Salvador, Gladys understands the balancing act a child learns in becoming bicultural and bilingual as well as how crucial literacy is in the development of an individual's success.

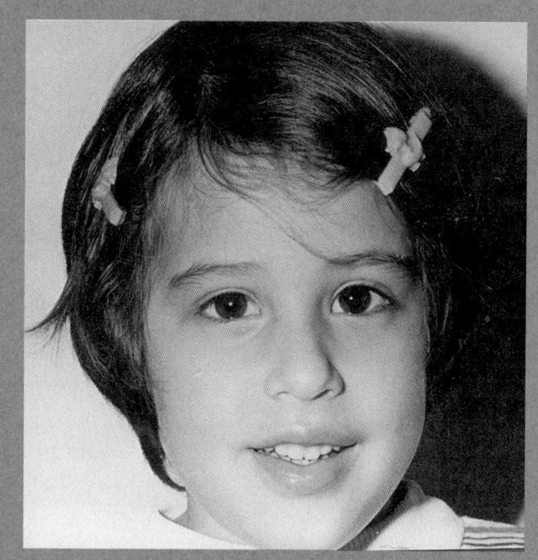